Dog Watch

BOOK FIVE

Extreme Stunt Dogs

Dog Watch

*Keeping the town of Pembrook
safe for people and dogs!*

Dog Watch

BOOK FIVE

Extreme Stunt Dogs

By Mary Casanova

Illustrated by Omar Rayyan

Aladdin Paperbacks

New York   London   Toronto   Sydney

ALADDIN PAPERBACKS
An imprint of Simon & Schuster Children's Publishing Division
1230 Avenue of the Americas, New York, NY 10020
Text copyright © 2007 by Mary Casanova
Illustrations copyright © 2007 by Omar Rayyan
All rights reserved, including the right of reproduction
in whole or in part in any form.
ALADDIN PAPERBACKS and related logo are registered
trademarks of Simon & Schuster, Inc.
Designed by Tom Daly
The text of this book was set in Gazette.
Manufactured in the United States of America
First Aladdin Paperbacks edition September 2007
2 4 6 8 10 9 7 5 3 1
Library of Congress Control Number 2007922979
ISBN-13: 978-1-4169-4782-0
ISBN-10: 1-4169-4782-5

Dedicated to

the dogs of Ranier, Minnesota—
past, present, and future

And

to Kate, Eric, and Charlie—
and to our family dogs, who have
brought us tears and trouble,
laughter and love
over the years

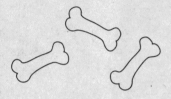

True:

On the edge of a vast northern Minnesota lake sits a quiet little village where dogs are allowed to roam free. Free, that is, until they get in trouble. One report of a tipped garbage can, nonstop barking, or car chasing, and the village clerk thumbs through *DOGGIE MUG SHOTS*, identifies the dog from its photo, and places a round sticker on the culprit's page. Then she phones the dog's owner. Too many stickers, and the troublesome dog is ordered to stay home—tethered to a chain or locked in its yard. No more roaming, no more adventures with the other dogs of the village.

The Big Truck Arrives

As on most sunny mornings, the dogs of Pembrook met at the fire hydrant outside the post office. This July morning was no different. All sniffs and wags—Kito, Chester, Schmitty, Tundra, Gunnar, and Muffin— were busy sharing the latest news when a sleek, white truck rolled past them. It slowed down, bumped over the curb across the street, and rumbled onto the empty field between Main Street and Seven Oaks Park. Kito studied the truck closely.

"Y'all see that?" Muffin said, twirling

around on her tiny back legs the way she always did when she got excited.

Gunnar replied in his deep basset hound voice, "Sure dooooo!"

Kito gazed across the street. He read the glittery gold and red words emblazoned across the long, white truck: HOLLYWOOD'S AMAZING EXTREME STUNT DOGS! What would fancy dogs like that be doing in Pembrook?

Chester lifted his beagle nose to the air. "A truckload of dogs! Maybe someone's opening up a pet store. It's about time we have more American Kennel Club registered dogs, besides me, in the village!"

"Hey, hotshot," Schmitty said, cocking his silky Labrador ears. "I came from a good litter. We may not be registered Labs, but we're still *great* dogs. A dog doesn't need fancy papers to be important. And I can fetch a stick with the best of 'em."

"Criminy biscuits," Chester said. "Tell that to those fancy dogs who win ribbons at the Westminster Dog Show. You think they let mutts into those shows? I think not." He pushed his snout skyward. "Someday I'll prove just how special my breeding is and—"

"Give it a rest," Schmitty said, and the two started going nose to nose.

"Hey, you two," Tundra said, who was always quick to bring order to their fighting. With her tall, white German shepherd body, she held her position as alpha dog quite easily. "Chester," she said, "enough."

"All I'm saying," Chester said, "is that my ancestors are from royalty. From across the seas in England. And my AKC papers—"

In a flash of teeth, Tundra pounced at Chester. He immediately rolled over on his back, paws and feet skyward, and offered her his neck. "I'm sorry! I'm sorry!"

Schmitty, too, pressed his whole body to the pavement, head upon his paws. Tundra turned to him next and hovered above him, a soft growl in her throat. "When I say 'enough,' I mean 'enough.'"

Then she turned toward Main Street, looked both ways before crossing, and led the gathering of dogs toward the truck.

Schmitty and Chester followed behind, tails tucked. Kito lagged, staying cautious.

A man in short, spiky hair and sunglasses jumped out of the driver's seat of the truck. He stretched, palms up to the sky. "So this is Pembrook," he said with a wide yawn, then glanced at the dogs. "Hey, doggy-dogs," he said. "Any of *you* wanna join my show? You'd have to prove yourself—only the best and the brightest in this operation."

Chester stood his tallest, which wasn't very tall, and puffed up his chest. "You're lookin' at him," he said. But of course, the man couldn't hear Chester's words. Silent language worked only between dogs.

Dogs or no dogs, until Kito knew this man better, he wasn't going to trust him. He was still a *stranger*, and strangers needed to be watched very, very carefully. Legs braced, back hairs stiff with warning, Kito growled at the man. *Grrrrr.*

The man backed up closer to his truck, grabbed a sheet of paper from inside, then pressed a few buttons on his cell phone and held it to his ear. "Mayor Jorgenson?" he said. "This is Mitch. We're here—ready to set up for tonight's show, man. But fundraiser or not," he said, staring at the dogs, "you gotta get these dogs around here on leashes! We can't do our show with uncontrolled dogs causing distractions. I've never seen so many. . . . What do you mean, a no-leash village?"

There was a pause.

"Really . . . okay, okay, man. That's good."

The dogs lingered around the truck, sniffing and listening. From inside the truck came the sound of several dogs whining, but it was so quiet, Kito wasn't sure if he'd imagined the sounds or not. If he'd just been traveling miles and miles in a truck, he'd be barking and whining loud enough so that someone would let him out. He studied the truck, with its long body and front cab. He couldn't imagine being cooped up like a chicken in a henhouse all day long, Hollywood glitter or not. He'd be anxious to get outside for some fresh air. But Mitch didn't seem concerned about letting his dogs out.

Villagers came and went. Some talked with Mitch. Kids arrived on bikes, many in their swimsuits, heading to the beach. They pointed at the truck and talked about coming back later for the stunt show. The village handyman, Mr. Cutler, arrived with tools and equipment to help set up. Soon, hot dog and popcorn stands sprang up too.

All the while, the dogs hovered, taking shelter in the shade of a tree or under the bleachers. Kito kept a keen eye on Mitch as he set up a white plastic fence and other mysterious equipment around the field. By late afternoon, every villager and dog in Pembrook knew the Extreme Stunt Dog Show was in town.

Village dogs finally grew hungry and wandered home. When Kito and Chester pawed at the front door of their cedar-sided house, Mrs. Hollinghorst welcomed them inside and set down two heaping bowls of Hearty Hound. "Okay, boys. Here you go."

Later, while the Hollinghorsts were reading the newspaper on the deck, Mrs. H said aloud, "With the preview show tonight, I see that Pembrook dogs will have to be on leashes. But just for tonight and during the big Friday performance."

Soon after, Mr. and Mrs. H snapped leashes on Kito and Chester. "Time to go check out the preview show."

Kito sunk all his weight onto his haunches. He sat, refusing to budge.

"Kito?" Mr. H said, giving the leash a tug. "Come along."

Reluctantly, he rose to his feet. "A leash?" he complained to Chester as they headed toward Pine Street. "In Pembrook! This isn't fair!"

"Hey, pal," Chester said, tail wagging. "Be a good sport. I'm sure Mighty Mitch has his reasons for wanting us on leashes. It's worth it, I'm sure."

Maybe Chester didn't mind, but to Kito, being leashed went completely against village policy. Well-behaved dogs were allowed to run free. Only dogs that got in trouble and received too many colored stickers on their page at the village clerk's office were supposed to be leashed. This wasn't fair! It was a breach of justice! And who was this Mighty Mitch, anyway? So what if he was from Hollywood? No amount of glitter was worth a dog's freedom.

A Taste of Greatness

The Hollinghorsts hurried for seats on the bleachers. To Kito's relief, they chose the bottom row, front and center. He didn't like slippery bleacher steps.

Just three feet away from where he sat, the field had been completely transformed. Rather than plain, mowed grass, the field was now set up as an obstacle course, brimming with colorful ladders and jumps, tunnels and tubes. Hoops of various sizes and heights were set up, one beside a plastic pool of water.

Kito's heart beat faster. He didn't know what to expect next.

In the center of the white-fenced field stood Mighty Mitch. Kito barely recognized him. Sparkly black sunglasses covered his eyes. He lifted his top hat off short, spiky blond hair. "Ladies and gentlemen! Boys and girls!" he began.

With a black tuxedo jacket over shorts and red sneakers, the man they'd met earlier strutted back and forth, shouting into the microphone. "My name is Mighty Mitch Tripline from L.A.—that's Los Angeles, Cal-i-forn-ia! And you lucky folks of Pembrook, Minn-e-so-ta, are about to witness Holly-wood's Amazing Extreme Stunt Dogs!"

From a black box the size of a refrigerator, rock music blared beside the stunt dog truck. It was so loud, Kito wished he could cover his ears. *Bum-bum-bumba-bum! Bum-bum-bumba-bum!*

"You've seen them on commercials! You've seen them in movies! You've watched them on late-night talk shows! And now, let the most amazing dogs in the world dance into your lives to steal your hearts away!"

Bum-bum-bumba-bum!Bum-bum-bumba-bum!

A murmur of anticipation rose from the crowd. Everyone in Pembrook had turned out. The bleachers were filled. The summer evening was free of a single overhead cloud. With a soft breeze from the lake, the weather couldn't have been better.

"I don't see why we have to be leashed," Chester said, suddenly trying to wiggle out of his collar.

"Hey, I thought you didn't mind."

"But this music! I want to twist and turn—dance about!"

Kito sat beside him. "Maybe Mighty Mitch thinks we'll outshine his wonder dogs. Hey, I don't like being on a leash either, but if it's only during the stunt shows, I guess I can live with it."

Bear, the Newfoundland dog in the village, sat at the feet of his owner, Angelica Phillips, whose reporter-ready camera was around her neck. Her pen was poised above her notepad. Bear glanced at Kito and Chester. "I'm not sure," he said, "but I think I may have seen this show somewhere in Canada last year."

"Really?" Chester asked. "Is it good?"

"I don't know. I was homeless then. All I cared about was finding something to eat." He glanced up at Angelica Phillips. "Things are better now."

Tundra sat by Mr. Harry Erickson, looking a little less alpha-like on her leather leash. Mr. Erickson hadn't bothered to change out of his butcher apron. He probably intended to leave his shop for as short a time as possible. But even *he* had made time for the show.

"This is the day you have all been waiting for!" Mighty Mitch continued. He strutted to an enclosed purple tent, lifted a flap, and said, "Let's hear it for the one, the only, the fastest dog in the world—"

The music blared. *Bum-bum-bumba-bum! Bum-bum-bumba-bum!*

"Tornado!!!"

Out sprinted the tiniest dog in the world.

It zipped over a bridge, climbed up a steep ladder and flew down the other side again, disappeared inside a long plastic tunnel and raced out the other end, then rounded the last part of the course—three tall jumps. And without missing a beat, the little Chihuahua cleared every pole and then jumped up into Mighty Mitch's arms.

"That's only the beginning, folks! Let's give the smallest member of Hollywood's Amazing Extreme Stunt Dogs a big, Pembrook round of applause!!! Let's hear it for Tornado!!!"

The crowd whistled, cheered, and clapped to the blaring music.

"Who knows," Mighty Mitch said with a sweep of his arm to the crowd. "Maybe even a Pembrook dog could become a stunt dog someday! At the big show, local dogs will get a chance to perform and do tricks too. It'll be lots of fun!" The villagers glanced around at the various dogs.

Muffin suddenly hopped on her hind legs and twirled in a circle. "Hollywood, here I come!" she yipped.

Chester danced at the end of his leash and placed his paws up on the edge of the plastic fence. "Pick me, pick me!" he whined.

Schmitty barked out, "I can jump higher and run faster than that little Chihuahua!"

And Gunnar, who was too fat to roll over most days, rolled over in the grass—not once, but *three* times in a row.

Kito held himself rigid. A shiver zigged from his nose to the tip of his fluffy chow chow tail. He didn't know why, but something told him that as long as the Extreme Stunt Dog show was in town, he'd better keep his wits about him. All this talk of Hollywood was going to some of the dogs' heads.

Dog Watch could not forget its true mission: *to keep the village safe for people and dogs.*

3

Fame and Fortune

After Mighty Mitch sent Tornado back into the purple tent, he announced: "And next, ladies and gentlemen, girls and boys, for your viewing pleasure, all the way from Hollywood, please help me welcome—"

Bum-bum-bumba-bum!Bum-bum-bumba-bum!

"Boomerang!!!"

Darting from the tent, a medium-size black dog with a tuft of white on its chest pranced about, and then sat obediently next to Mighty Mitch, watching for his command.

"Looks like a sheepherding dog," Kito said.

"Probably a mixed-breed," Chester said with an air of superiority.

Mighty Mitch looked pointedly around at the audience, as if daring anyone to prove him wrong. "Now Boomerang can *outjump*, *outcatch* any dog out there."

"Yeah, right," Schmitty said, straining at the end of his leash. "I'd show that pampered pup about fetching and jumping."

From his tuxedo coat, Mighty Mitch produced a bright green Frisbee. "Now the way we train our dogs," he explained, "is we *reward* them with what they love. Rewards—not punishment. And there's nothing that Boomerang loves more than—you guessed it—this Frisbee!"

Schmitty glanced to Kito. "I'm the best at catching Frisbees. If I just had a chance out there . . . I'd prove it!"

"I'm sure you could," Kito shot back.

Then Mighty Mitch and Boomerang sprang into their performance. Mighty Mitch tossed one Frisbee straight up into the sky, which Boomerang watched intently. Before it landed, Mighty Mitch reached into his tuxedo and tossed another Frisbee, then another and another. With his four feet off the ground, Boomerang caught the first Frisbee, then flew after the others, jumping and catching them in midair—dropping one Frisbee to catch the next.

Kito felt exhausted just watching the dog. He wondered what kind of reward would ever make him work that hard. Certainly not a Frisbee. Maybe a bowl of Hearty Hound— or treats, like Liver Snaps.

Next, Mighty Mitch lay on his back, and as Boomerang ran at him, the trainer tossed a Frisbee straight into the air. Boomerang shot up directly into the air above Mitch's body, caught the Frisbee, and miraculously landed just inches away from Mitch and not directly on him.

"That was good," Chester said.

In the next second, Mighty Mitch was back on his feet, leaning outward, clenching the edge of a Frisbee in his teeth, which Boomer-ang ran at and—midair—snatched away.

"Let's give a huge round of applause, ladies and gentlemen, girls and boys, for one of the dog wonders of the world—Boomerang!"

Bum-bum-bumba-bum!Bum-bum-bumba-bum!

The audience went wild with clapping and whistling.

Chester flopped on the ground, head between his paws. Kito scooted over closer. "You were all excited just a few seconds ago," he said. "What's wrong, buddy? Sick?"

"I was made for this," Chester said.

"For what, exactly?"

"Good giblets, Kito! For this! For fame and fortune. For stardom. And here I sit, wasting away my true talents in this little northern village. Hollywood is out there. Someone out there is looking for a beagle to star in some-thing—I just know it. A beagle with talent, smarts, and ability . . ."

Kito figured it was better to just listen and not say a word.

"I think this is my time," Chester said. "Start with the stunt show, then get picked up by a talent scout. But if this show moves on before I get noticed, then I'll have missed my chance. I have to come up with a way to prove myself—and fast."

"Wait just a second," Kito said. "You're saying, after watching those two stunt dogs, that you'd throw away your life here in Pembrook, throw away your part in keeping the village safe, and go on the road?"

"Righto. In a heartbeat."

"But, Chester, you don't know what really goes on behind the scenes. You don't know what's going on in that tent, in that truck. You don't know how those dogs really live."

"Do I need to? C'mon, Kito! You heard the applause! You saw those dogs zip around like they were having the time of their lives! What's to question?" He sat up and looked Kito squarely in the eyes. "You know, Mr. Serious, I think that sometimes you just don't know what it means to follow your dreams. To go after the big time. I feel it in my bones.

I was meant to be a stunt dog—a star dog."

Kito couldn't believe how seriously Chester was taking all of this. He didn't know what to say.

"If you were a real friend, Kito, you'd support me. You'd encourage me to give it a try. To reach for the stars! But, no. You just give me that old stare-down, warning me to be careful. Well, not this time. I'm going for it. I just have to figure out how."

"I'm your friend, you know that, Chester."

"Well then, support me. I need to get in that spotlight." He motioned with his snout to the field again, where Mighty Mitch was pointing again to the tent curtain.

"Friday's evening show, ladies and gentlemen, will be even greater. Two nights from now, you'll be treated to a full stunt show. This was just a teaser. So spread the word! Bring everyone you can. A portion of your entrance fee of twenty dollars goes to the national program I started called Help a Dog in Need. Every dollar you contribute goes directly to the care and well-being of dogs who are homeless and in shelters around the country. Also, I'll be offering a brand-new dog product! So good night, and I'll see you all back here in two days!"

The music blared, and the crowd cheered.

"Hear that?" Chester said. "People pay twenty dollars to see these shows. That would buy lots of dog food for other dogs in need."

"Yeah, I heard," Kito answered, yet he still didn't like this Mighty Mitch guy. Maybe it was the way he dressed and talked, or the big ring that glinted on his hand, but Kito sensed it was more than that. It was the way he flagged Kito's back hairs and set him on edge.

The crowd was thinning and heading home, but Mr. and Mrs. H lingered to visit with friends. Kito and Chester sat, waiting.

"That's fine for those dogs," Mrs. H said to Harry Erickson, the grocer, "but we love our dogs being at home with us." The grocer took off his white butcher's cap, scratched his head of thin, white hair, then put his cap back on again.

"I can't picture Tundra doin' those fancy stunts. Bet it's a hard life being on the road like that."

"See?" Kito said to Chester. "It's not perfect out there."

"Chicken livers! What do they know? I bet those stunt dogs get applause wherever they go!" He turned his black button nose toward the obstacle course, now empty of dogs. Only Mitch was outside now, signing autographs.

Chester, his tail pointed straight out—a sure sign he was intent on some sort of mission—said, "I'm coming back tonight. I'm going to try that course and start practicing. I'll show all of Pembrook just what I can do!"

Kito didn't want to dampen his buddy's dream, but he doubted that Chester was really stunt dog material. "So, what's going to be your special talent?"

"Slobbering salami chunks! I don't know yet. I haven't thought that far ahead. But I'll figure out a way."

Then it struck Kito: If he went along with

Chester, he'd be accomplishing two things. First, he'd be showing his friend that he cared. And second, while Chester practiced stunts, he'd snoop around the Extreme Stunt Dog Show tent and truck. There was something about this whole operation that just didn't sit right with him. Why did he continue to hear the faint sound of whining and barking from within the truck? If it was such a good life, why weren't the show dogs lounging around on the grass outside? Maybe the show dogs didn't want to be surrounded by fans, but still, Kito needed to find out more.

He needed to investigate.

4

Competition Heats Up

On leashes, the dogs walked back on Pine Street, the pavement still warm under Kito's paws.

"Even though you don't have to be leashed again until Friday's show, you boys should stick around home," Mrs. H said as she unsnapped them. "Those stunt dogs might need to practice without being disturbed."

"Criminy crackers!" Chester said to Kito. "That's an idea. We'll head back and talk with the stars. They might be able to give me some tips on getting started."

Kito couldn't take it anymore. He dashed to the lake to cool off. The water soothed his overheated paws. All that blaring music and talk of Hollywood had made his skin itchy and his feet sweaty. He waded out until the water dampened his underbelly and eased away his stress. As part chow chow, he wasn't bred for water. His thick coat could keep him warm in a blizzard, but once it was wet, it took hours to dry off. Still, he couldn't resist a good belly cooldown once in a while.

Several yards away, at the end of the neighbor's dock, Schmitty went flying through the air after a stick. He landed, head above water, and swam for the stick.

"Good boy!" Hillary Rothchild called from the dock, her gardens in full bloom behind her.

Enjoying the cool water, Kito watched Schmitty dog-paddle as if his life depended on it. When the Lab reached shore, he shook out his coat and delivered the stick to his owner.

"Thatta boy, Schmitty!" A round, straw

hat topped off Hillary's silky black hair and pale skin. Usually on her hands and knees in her gardens, weeding and planting, she kept her yard fenced so that other dogs didn't "do their business," as Schmitty once explained. Her gardens were thick with flowers and ferns, trees and vines, covering every inch of her house and yard. Along the shore, her lilies flaunted their colors of bright yellow and pink. To Kito, Hillary Rothchild seemed an unlikely owner for a black Lab, but Schmitty had explained that she'd fallen in love with him as a puppy and, ever since, she'd let him sleep on her bed.

"You never tire of retrieving, do you?" Hillary said, stick in hand again.

Schmitty sat on his rump, his body wiggled from his black tail to his black nose. He was ready to fetch.

Kito, however, let out a big sigh and let the waters of the big lake work away his worries. The stress of the Extreme Stunt Dog Show eased from his shoulders. His tight brow began to relax. Only two more days and the show would be gone. The big white truck with the fancy gold and red lettering would head down the road to the next town. All this hype about dogs starring in commercials and Hollywood movies was making some of the Pembrook dogs—Muffin, Schmitty, Gunnar, and Chester, in particular—act strange. Sugarcoated dreams of stardom were dancing in their heads. Wasn't it enough to be a good dog? A dog that guarded hearth and home? A member of Dog Watch?

"Ready, Schmitty?" Hillary said, her arm back, ready to throw the stick.

Schmitty's tail thumped on the dock.

The stick flew, and Schmitty leaped through the air. He landed in the water, but the stick didn't. It landed on Kito's dock.

He glanced out at Schmitty, who swam in wider and wider circles, looking for the stick. Kito wanted to tell him where the stick was, but he was too far away to hear. Silent language between dogs has its limits.

Chester trotted down to the lake and stood on the dock above Kito. "What's up?"

"Coolin' off,'" Kito replied, happy to stay in the comfortable water.

"Schmitty!" Hillary called out, pointing to the Hollinghorsts' dock. "Over there!"

But Schmitty swam farther and farther into the bay. The sun was sinking lower and sprinkling the bay's surface with dazzling flecks of gold. What if Schmitty kept looking for the stick long into the night?

"Look at him," Chester said. "You'd think he was trying to win a swimming record. What's he after?"

"A stick—but it landed on our dock. He'll never find it."

At that, Chester put his nose to the ground. *Snuffle, snuff, snuff.* He wound his way from the sandy shore to the top of the dock, right to the stick, which he snapped up.

"Ha! Got it! And he said he could fetch anything. Just proves that there's probably only room for one Pembrook dog in that stunt show, and I'll bet you anything it's going to be a registered beagle."

"Oh, brother."

Head high, Chester trotted toward the deck, where Mr. and Mrs. H were seated in slatted wooden chairs, reading. He dropped the stick at their feet.

"Chester," Mr. H said, putting down his book, "you want me to throw this?"

Worried, Kito scanned the bay. Schmitty was still paddling in circles. He had to do something to stop his searching. Seagulls floated overhead with questioning cries.

He stepped out of the water, gave his coat a good shake, and then dashed up to where Chester was sitting. He sat right beside him, nose pointed to the stick.

"You two don't usually like to play fetch," Mr. H said, one eyebrow inching up. "Did that stunt show motivate you?" He chuckled to himself, as if it was the farthest thing from a dog's thoughts. "Okay," he said, rising from his chair. "I'll throw it, if you like." He tossed the stick and it flew through the air above the grass, out over the dock, and into the water with a splash. "Oops. Guess I don't know my own strength!"

The dogs took off for the stick, nearly tackling one another in the process, and stopped abruptly at the end of their dock.

One seagull, then several, swooped closer to the stick, then rose to the sky, their cries mournful. They had probably hoped it was old bread scraps or fish scraps. No such luck.

The stick bobbed in the lake.

"I'm not jumping in after it," Chester said. "What does he think I am, a Labrador retriever?"

"No," Kito said, "but here comes one."

From out in the middle of the bay, Schmitty dog-paddled closer and closer, his breathing labored. "There . . . it . . . is! I've been looking everywhere for that stick!" Then he clamped the stick in his pink mouth and paddled off with it toward home.

"Hey!" Chester barked out, "That's *my* stick! Finders keepers! Besides, it might become part of my show!" He took off along the shore toward Schmitty's dock.

"Here comes trouble," Kito mumbled under his breath.

Schmitty heaved himself out of the lake and up onto his dock. Hillary clapped her hands for him. "Good boy! I was worried!"

The moment Schmitty dropped the stick to shake out his black coat, Chester darted from the nearby bush, snatched the stick, and ran off with it. His hind legs propelled him like a jack rabbit outrunning a fox.

"You stinking little beagle!" Schmitty barked, his back hairs bristling. "I was in training! That's *my* stick!" He bolted after Chester, and they both disappeared into Hillary's lovely botanical gardens.

A torrent of growling and yelping followed.

"Hey!" yelled Hillary Rothchild. "Stop it you two, before you kill one another! And my gardens—stop it! You'll ruin the hostas and primroses!"

Kito glanced up at the Hollinghorsts, who had abandoned their chairs and books and were running toward the snarling and growling. Kito dashed after them. He had to try to break up the fight before one of his buddies got hurt.

Until Mighty Mitch Tripline and his traveling dogs left Pembrook, he had the gut feeling that life for village dogs would get worse before it got better.

Chester's Longing

"Chester!" Mrs. H shouted. "It's just a stupid stick. Stop fighting!"

Hillary Rothchild squared her pale hands to her tiny waist. "Schmitty. Sit!"

But Schmitty and Chester were eyeball to eyeball, each clamping firmly on his end of the stick.

Instinctively, Kito wanted to join in, but he held back—and Mr. H's firm hand on his collar helped.

A droplet of blood mixed with Chester's drool. Schmitty's paw left a red stain on the grass. They pulled and snarled. Finally, Hillary grabbed her green hose and aimed the nozzle right at the stick. The dogs whined, then finally let go and slunk away toward their owners, dripping wet.

"I'm so sorry," Mrs. H said, bending down to grab Chester's collar. "I'm not sure what got into him."

Kito looked to Chester, then to Schmitty, only a few yards away. "You two are so revved up, trying to prove that you're hotshots, that you nearly killed each other. Don't you think you have better things to do?"

"I was practicing my retrieving skills," Schmitty said, "when this little twerp stole my prop."

"Prop?" Kito repeated. "It's a stick, Schmitty."

"Well," Chester said, his chest puffed out, "you can do only one thing, Schmitty. I not only can track down any scent, I can fetch sticks, too. I can even sing 'Jingle Bells' to the piano. And there's more where those skills come from!"

Schmitty humphed, then stretched his head toward his owner's hand. Hillary scratched him behind his ear, and Schmitty leaned into it. "Mmmm. There, that's good."

While Mr. and Mrs. H complimented Hillary on her beautiful gardens, the dogs talked.

"Schmitty," Kito said, "I think it's time for Dog Watch to sniff around that stunt show operation. Wouldn't you agree that things might not be *quite* what they seem? I mean, those dogs were locked in that truck for hours before the show began. Didn't you hear them whining?"

"Ah, nope," Schmitty replied. "All I saw, pal, was a golden future—a golden future for the world's most amazing Labrador retriever!" His tail swished back and forth across the grass. "I can hear it now! Ladies and gentlemen, boys and girls—the fastest, the best at fetching and—"

"Oh, stop. Not you, too!"

Then he felt a tug at his neck. "C'mon boys," Mr. H said, leading Kito by the collar. "I think you'd better come in for the night. It's getting quite late. Time for bed."

With his front feet off the ground and Mrs. H's hand on his collar, Chester glanced at Kito. "I proved I had the nose, didn't I? Schmitty didn't find that stick. I did!"

"Oh, give it up, Chester. Now you've blown it. We can't even go to the obstacle course because of your amazing behavior. A dogfight? That could lead to a sticker on your chart. Lucky for you, Schmitty's owner didn't mention wanting to report you."

"Jumpin' poodles. I didn't think of that. If I get another sticker and have to be locked or chained up at home, then how would I run away with the show?"

Kito looked on. "Did you say *run away*?"

The Hollinghorsts opened the door, and the dogs went inside ahead of them. "Let's check your mouth for wounds," Mrs. H said, wetting a paper towel and then kneeling in front of Chester.

"Open wide," Mrs. H said, forcing Chester's mouth open. She blotted his tongue, which must have been dangling during the big fight.

"Did you?" Kito pressed.

"*Run* away? Ah . . . no. I think I said I'd have *fun* away. You know, just have fun practicing at that obstacle course. I wouldn't *run* away. Now why would I want to do that?"

A Mouse in the House

The next morning, despite a soothing light breeze off the lake and the gentle sound of water lapping against the shore, Kito paced the living room floor. Chester was *definitely* covering up. It drained him to think that his buddy would consider running off with a show. But when Chester got an idea into his tiny, little brain, there was no telling what he might do. If Dog Watch could somehow prove that life on the road with Mighty Mitch wasn't perfect, then maybe he could keep Chester from doing something truly stupid.

Just then, Mrs. H screamed.

Kito sprang into his defensive posture: back hairs raised, all paws on the floor, and braced for trouble.

"A mouse in the house!" she cried.

A little grayish-brown mouse sat on the braided carpet beside the couch, nibbling on a piece of dog food.

"Insult of insults!" Chester said. He dashed after the rodent, but the mouse disappeared underneath the bulky furniture.

"Kito," Mrs. H said, "aren't you going to try and get it?"

Kito stood there. Mice left him uninspired. He was really bred to protect his family from larger dangers—like *strangers*. He was content to watch the spectacle.

Chester bayed at full pitch, his snout wedged under the couch, his rump in the air, and his tail up and wagging. But the mouse simply scurried out and across the hardwood floor. It shot up the wooden leg of the dining room table and sat on top, its tiny paws up against its chest.

Mrs. H opened the sliding door to the deck. "Chester, chase it out!"

Chester jumped up and down beside the table, his ears flaring out sideways with each jump. The mouse ran this way and that, zigging and zagging, clearly uncertain which way to go. Finally, it flew like a rocket off the table and shot toward the open door. Chester raced after it.

Kito darted after Chester. What if he ran away?!

"Good boy, Chester!" Mrs. H exclaimed, standing behind Kito on the deck. The mouse must have found a hole to disappear into, because Chester soon lost its trail. But Chester wasn't idle for long.

A red squirrel circled the base of a nearby cedar tree, and careening this way and that, nose to the ground, Chester tracked it. When he spotted the squirrel halfway up the tree, Chester ran with amazing speed and raced toward the trunk, as if he would run right up it. *And he did!* He darted up a few feet, and then in a full backflip, landed on the ground on all four feet.

"Barking beef burgers!" he called. "Kito, did you see *that*?!"

Mrs. H called for her husband. "Honey, come here—quick! You won't believe what Chester just did!"

Kito was certain that Chester could never do the same trick twice. It was sheer luck, his hunting instincts on overdrive. A freak accident of an overeager beagle. Still, it was doggone amazing

"C'mon, Chester," Mrs. H coaxed, looking on from the deck. "Do it again!"

"Maybe you were seeing things," Mr. H said doubtfully.

"C'mon, Chester," she called.

On a high branch, the squirrel churred a nasty warning to Chester, who sat at the tree's base, his nose upward. Again, he stepped back, ran for the tree, ran up the trunk a few feet, did his backflip, and landed.

Mr. and Mrs. H clapped.

With applause, Chester repeated his

performance over and over again to the Hollinghorsts' laughter and cheering.

Kito had to admit, it was a pretty good stunt.

Too good.

"Cal-i-for-nia," Chester sang, ready to perform again, "here I come!"

Before Chester was done with his backflip performance, and while the Hollinghorsts were busy clapping, Kito trotted off. Rarely did he set off on his own, but with Chester so preoccupied with becoming a stunt dog, he had to go it alone. He needed to snoop around Mighty Mitch's operation before his buddy ran away with stunt dog dreams of fame and fortune. If he didn't figure it out soon, it might be too late.

Snoopin' Around

The mid-morning sun beat down on Kito's back. His thick undercoat of hair trapped the heat until his tongue hung loose. He paused in the shade of the community building. He spotted Gunnar across the street at the tavern, also in the shade. But he was rolling over and over.

Despite the heat, Kito trotted over to Gunnar's side.

"Did you get stung by hornets?" he asked.

"Hiiiiiii. I'm working on myyyy trick."

"And what trick is that?" Kito asked wearily.

"It's called 'stop, drop, and roll.' Seeee?" He stood up on his short, thick legs, which didn't lift his large body very far from the pavement. "This is—'stop.'" Then he drooped slowly to his belly. "This is—'drop.'" And then he rolled slowly three times and stopped, his short, stocky legs pointed toward the sky. "And—'roll.'"

Without moving, he glanced at Kito. "Sooo, saaay something. Is it gooood?"

"Great," Kito said without much enthusiasm. "But what's wrong with just being a normal dog in Pembrook? I suppose you're thinking of joining that stunt show too?"

Gunnar closed his eyes. "Noooo harm in dreeeeaming."

"But what about Dog Watch? What if every dog left to become a stunt dog? Then what? What about our motto: '*Day or night, Pembrook dogs unite*'?"

The door to the tavern opened. Gunnar rose to his feet and slipped inside without an answer.

With a long sigh, Kito headed toward the post office and the fire hydrant painted like

Raggedy Ann. He remembered when they'd formed Dog Watch. It had started when Tundra had gone missing, when trouble had begun springing up like brushfires around the village, faster than the dogs could put them out. That's when they had decided it was better to work together to keep their village safe. As a team, they could do a better job than by working alone.

Kito looked around. Alone at the fire hydrant. Not a dog to be seen. He studied the long, white, glittering truck across the street. Its red and gold letters shimmered in the sun. On the truck's south side, an awning stretched over the fenced area. Under the awning, Mighty Mitch leaned back in a lounge chair, feet outstretched, an icy drink in one hand, an open book in the other. But still no sign of his stunt dogs. Did the dogs live their whole lives in the truck, except for the fleeting moments during the show? Just when *did* the dogs get out to just be dogs? Things didn't feel right.

It would be far better to investigate under the cover of darkness, but Kito couldn't count on getting out at night. On summer evenings, the sun stayed high in the sky, sometimes past the late evening news. With the show tomorrow, he didn't have the luxury of time. There was no telling how many dogs might try to leave with the stunt show.

Slowly, like a cat stalking a bird, Kito moved alongside the white plastic fencing that marked the obstacle course. Step by slow step, paws lost in the green grass, he made his way toward the awning, where Mighty Mitch was sitting on a lounge chair. If he moved slowly enough, he hoped Mighty Mitch Tripline wouldn't spot him.

"Hey, you!" Mighty Mitch called. "Chow chows are pretty smart dogs. So what are you up to, fella?"

Instantly, Kito's back hairs went pencil-straight. He stopped, with only two yards and a white plastic fence between himself and Mighty Mitch. "I could use a dog like you in my show. Got any special talents? Baton twirling, perhaps?" Mighty Mitch chuckled at his own wit. He lifted up his book. "Reading, maybe?" He laughed again.

If he only knew, Kito thought. The title on the book cover caught his eye: *Dog Magic: How to Make Your Dog Do Whatever You Ask*. The title wasn't surprising, but its author was. Beneath the title were the words "By famous dog trainer, Mighty Mitch Tripline."

Kito's stomach twisted. He could understand a dog trainer reading up on how to better do his job. But what kind of author spends time reading his own book?

"Here," Mighty Mitch said, reading from the book. "When your dog is reluctant to perform, simply make his rewards *more* rewarding.

In other words, through rewards—never punishments—find ways to help your dog discover *gratitude*."

Kito had to admit, a trainer who only used rewards and not punishments sounded good. So why was his gut still tight with caution?

Mighty Mitch glanced at Kito and laughed. "You're a funny dog, you know that? You look at me like you're really listening. Want to hear more?"

Kito stared, hoping for more.

"For example, if a dog is not taking easily to house breaking and he's piddling in places around the house where you don't want him to go, you need to put in place the Gratitude Program. If he's not holding it when you're away from home and you return to soiled carpets—his reward? Not treats. Not biscuits. But the *opportunity* to go outside and do his business. And how do you make that a reward? By keeping the dog confined in a small crate until he's absolutely desperate to get out. And then, and only then, do you take your dog directly from its crate to the outdoors. This way, he can't make a mistake. You're happy. He's happy. Especially when you praise him."

Mighty Mitch glanced up with a sly smile and added, "Yeah, especially when you reward him with Mighty Miscuits."

Kito stared. Mighty Miscuits? What were those? Biscuits? Something that Mighty Mitch gave to his dogs?

"Ah, Mighty Miscuits," Mitch said, swirling the ice cubes around in his glass, his green ring stone glinting. "They are truly the magic in this business," he said with a wink. Then he drained his glass, set it beside him in the grass, leaned back in his chair and, with his arms behind his head, closed his eyes.

There was something in all this that Kito knew was important, yet he couldn't make sense of it. But his gut told him to find out more and, when he had enough dirt on this Mighty Mitch, to round up Dog Watch for an emergency meeting.

Until then, however, all he had was . . . was . . .

A gut feeling.

Bella

While Mighty Mitch Tripline napped in the shade, Kito slipped stealthily under the big truck. He might be able to use dog language to communicate with the dogs inside, unless the truck's floor was made of cement.

"Hey!" he called, his head touching the dirty underside of the long vehicle. He heard no response. He tried again. "Hey! Anybody in there?"

"Yes, darling!" came the reply. It was a soft-voiced dog of good breeding, Kito guessed. Maybe a female poodle. "Lots of us! We've been in this truck for endless hours—maybe even days! When is he going to let us out? Does he think we can hold it forever?"

"Hold it? You mean—"

"You heard me."

"Is that part of his 'Gratitude Program'?"

"You know about that? Yes, darling! He keeps us so miserably caged that when he finally lets us out to a patch of grass, we'll do anything he asks—just to gain a few moments of freedom from this prison!"

"Y'know, I had a bad feeling," Kito began, "but I promise. I'll do what I can to—"

"You! Chow-dog!" Mighty Mitch was crouched beside the truck and peering in at Kito. "Get outta there! Right now! I was taking a sweet little nap, and you've got my dogs whining when they should be silent."

Suddenly, Mighty Mitch had a small container in his hand and shot a mist of something directly into Kito's eyes.

"Ha! Nothing a little spray won't fix!"

Blinded, Kito darted away from Mighty Mitch and out from under the truck. His eyes watered, stung, and burned. Tail between his legs, he ran bleary-eyed past the community building, down Pine Street, and home.

How mean! What harm had he caused? He didn't deserve such harsh treatment. He pawed at the front door until it opened. And when it did, Mrs. H dropped to her knees. "Kito, Kito. What's wrong with your eyes? You can barely open them!" He whimpered in reply.

When he should have been calling an emergency Dog Watch meeting, when he should have been working to help the confined stunt dogs, when he should have been finding out more about Mighty Miscuits and the foul "Gratitude Program," Kito instead found himself wasting time in the waiting room of the vet's office.

His eyelids were heavy with puffiness. Though the burning sensation was gone, his eyes were watery and sore.

A stream of dogs and cats went in and out of the vet's office ahead of him.

"Oh, what a beautiful dog," one man commented in the waiting room. "But, his eyes. Oh dear, they look awful. Are chow chow eyes meant to look like that?"

Kito rested his head on Mrs. H's lap. He didn't want to be studied by *strangers*, especially when he could barely see them!

Finally, his turn came. "Kito," the vet said, holding a clipboard against her chest and over her braids. "What seems to be the problem?"

Mrs. H replied. "I don't really know. He was fine earlier, then he showed up at the door nearly blind."

On the cold examination table, Kito sat patiently as the vet checked his ears, took his temperature, asked questions about his diet, looked in his eyes with a small flashlight, ran tests, and finally returned to the exam room and pronounced: "Pepper spray."

"Pepper spray?" Mrs. H repeated. "But who would do such a thing?"

"Someone who doesn't like dogs, I suppose."

"In Pembrook? That doesn't make any sense. Everybody in Pembrook loves dogs, otherwise they'd live somewhere else." Her brow furrowed, and anger crisscrossed her forehead in lines. "Why would someone do something so mean?"

The vet shook her head. "You know. Some people are simply not kind. Or, in this case, perhaps someone was afraid of Kito. Could he have been acting in a threatening manner?"

"It's possible. He's defensive around strangers. Perhaps a tourist cornered him and didn't know better. I suppose he might have scared someone—but pepper spray. It seems so excessive."

Kito groaned. If he could only tell them. He wasn't the threat. It was the grand and glorious Mighty Mitch. Stunt dog abuser. Dog meanie. Dog criminal!

"I suggest you keep an eye on him and let me know if his eye condition worsens. But I think this will pass—as long as he doesn't come in contact again with pepper spray anytime soon, that is. Say, are you going to Friday night's stunt dog show? Everybody's been talking about the preview. The full show should really be something."

"Definitely! I think our beagle, Chester, is inspired! He started doing backflips today."

The vet's eyebrows rose as a smile came to her lips. "You're putting me on."

"No, honest. He went after a squirrel, raced up the tree, and backflipped to his feet. I really must take him over to show that dog trainer. I think even *he* would be impressed!"

"Just so he doesn't steal Chester for his show," the vet said with a laugh.

"Oh, we'd never part with him, no matter what kind of tricks he comes up with. Still, it's pretty amazing."

Kito groaned. If she only knew. Chester's loyalty apparently ran only glitter-deep.

On the ride home, Kito had more than enough to worry about. Not only did he have to keep Chester from running away, but now he seriously worried that Mighty Mitch might offer Chester a part once he saw his backflip. Or steal him. If a guy could be so quick to use pepper spray, and so slow at letting dogs out to do their normal business, there was no telling what he was capable of.

Round-Up

When Kito returned home that afternoon, he headed straight for the couch where Chester was snoring. All that superdog behavior must have worn his buddy out. Kito touched him, nose to nose.

"Hey," he said. "Wake up. We've got real trouble brewing."

Chester opened one eye, then the other. "Wh-what's that?"

"Dog Watch. We need to round up everyone for a meeting."

"Oh," Chester said, arching his back and

stretching deeply. "I don't know about Dog Watch anymore." Then he bounded off the couch and began wiggling with energy. "I have to practice! Backflips are only the beginning. I mean, there's no telling about the depths of my talent. You go ahead without me this time."

Kito growled. Somebody had to knock some sense into that beagle. He charged Chester and tackled him until his buddy was flat on his back, his neck exposed.

Kito stood over him, glowering. He knew it was Tundra's job to be the alpha, the top dog, of the pack, but on occasion, he had to act like second in command, which most of the time he was.

"Okay," Chester said meekly, "I can practice after the meeting."

"Good."

"Smackin' biscuits!" Chester said. "Your eyes are all red and swollen. You been cryin' human tears?"

"I was attacked by your dream trainer with pepper spray, that's what."

"Attacked? You gotta be kidding. Mighty Mitch loves dogs. He knows how to bring out their best potential. He wouldn't—"

"Chester. Please. Just don't talk. For now, just follow, okay?"

Kito turned away, hoping Chester would follow. He pawed at the front door, whined, then barked.

Finally, book in hand, Mr. H let the dogs outside. He called after them, "Kito, you stay outta trouble out there."

Kito paused and looked at Mr. H. He tried to assure him by wagging his tail, but his tail drifted more toward the ground than up over his back. He needed his confidence back, and soon. The pepper spray encounter had hurt him in more ways than one.

Leading the way, Kito passed by Schmitty's house and its tidy gardens. Schmitty was on his deck, chewing the coveted stick. "What's up?" he called.

"Dog Watch!" Kito replied.

In one leap, Schmitty bounded over his picket fenced yard toward them. Good old

Schmitty. He didn't always need to ask questions.

Together, the three dogs raced to the post office—Schmitty and Chester trying to outpace each other.

"Bet I'm faster than that Boomerang!" Schmitty called as he tore ahead.

With the hind leg power of a kangaroo, Chester powered up and caught up to the lab. "Bet I'm even faster than you!"

Kito lagged behind and kept a steady pace. He caught up with them at the fire hydrant, their tongues hanging out. Gathering a deep, full breath, Kito sat squarely on his haunches and started barking: *"Day or night! Pembrook dogs unite!"*

Soon, especially since barking was so hard to resist once one dog started, Schmitty and Chester joined in.

"Day or night! Pembrook dogs unite!"

Before long, dogs emerged from every corner of the village. To Kito's relief, Tundra trotted from the grocery store, over the railroad tracks, to meet up with everyone. Kito felt himself relax a little. When their alpha dog was on board, everything went better.

As she approached, Chester whispered to Kito, "This better not be a false alarm. I have tricks to work on."

"Chester!" Kito warned under his breath. "Give it a rest!"

With dogs gathered in a tight circle around the hydrant, Tundra wove in and out among them, her white German shepherd body strong and imposing. "Who put out the alert?"

"I did," Kito answered.

"Then tell us," she said.

"The dogs that are part of Mighty Mitch's show are being confined for long periods in cages. They rarely get outside, and when they do, the dogs are so desperate that they'll do anything to please him. It's part of his Gratitude Program and—"

"Wait. The dogs live in the truck," Tundra said. "And what exactly do you think we can do about that?"

"I don't know yet. We need to find out

more. But something really stinks about his operation. I mean, he sprayed me in the eyes with pepper spray."

Muffin gasped. "Oh, honey, you poor, poor thing!"

Kito tried to wag away her comment. "Really, I'm fine. I'm okay now. But I was just trying to talk with his dogs, and he blasted me. Is that humane?"

"Well, maaaaybe his super dogs neeeeed their rest," Gunnar said. "They're not nooooormal dogs like us. They're shooooow dogs."

"Maybe they need special protection. Well . . ." he looked around. "We're riffraff compared to those dogs."

"Hey, speak for yourself!" Chester puffed out his chest. "He might be interested in taking *me* on tour. I mean, I *am* AKC registered, and did I tell you about my latest talent?"

"Sugar," Muffin said, slipping up under Chester's chin. "Tell us."

"Save it," Tundra said.

Muffin and Chester took two steps away

from Tundra as she loomed closer. "I think Kito's concerns are worth looking into. But we don't have much time. Only two nights until the big show, and then they'll be on their way."

She glanced over at the field. "Well, look over there."

The other dogs followed her gaze. And then, as one, they set off behind her to get closer.

The back doors of Mighty Mitch's truck were wide open.

Outside, within the fenced field, a dozen dogs raced about. They jumped and skidded and wrestled. Mighty Mitch was smiling from ear to ear. "That's my good dogs!" he called. "A few more minutes, then it's time to head back in."

"See?" Kito whispered. "They just got out."

"But they do look happy," Tundra said. "I mean, look at them."

Kito tried to spot the dog he'd talked to. She'd called him "darling." And he was almost certain that she was a poodle. But he didn't see anything that looked like a poodle . . . until his search stopped at a pink dog.

"Pink?" he said out loud.

"Isn't that just like showbiz?" Muffin squealed. "I wish-oh-wish that my owner would think about dyeing my coat some sweet, fun color like pink!"

The pink poodle looked toward Kito, then trotted to the edge of the fence. "Hey, darling!" she called out.

Schmitty and Chester looked at each other. Bear glanced away. Lucky raised her floppy golden retriever ears. "Who's she talking to?" she asked.

Kito didn't answer. Before Mighty Mitch could command his dogs back inside the truck, Kito raced to the fence. "What's your name?"

"Bella," she said. "And yours?"

"Kito."

"Oh, yes. I recognize your voice. Are you going to help us?"

Kito didn't know *how*, or even *what* he could

do. The Pembrook dogs clustered around him at the fence. The stunt dogs raced toward the gathering. Some were shaggy, others sleek. Most looked thin and fit, but a few were limping. A few started barking, then the Pembrook dogs barked back. Pretty soon, it was hard to hear anything. Kito tried to listen extra hard.

"You promised—"

"What did I promise?" he shouted. "I mean, what do you want?"

"Get me out of this show, darling," she said. "I want a real home. I want to escape."

"I'll do what I can, but here in Pembrook—"

"What did you say, darling?"

"With Dog Watch," he shouted, "I'm sure we can help you somehow."

Kito tried to picture a pink dog in Pembrook. If he helped Bella escape, would anyone want her? She was so different. But at least she was clearly a poodle, with wiry hair, which meant she didn't shed much or cause allergies—qualities that people spoke highly about whenever poodles were discussed.

But before he could say another word, Mighty Mitch came running at him with the can of pepper spray. Kito wasn't going to stick around to find out what getting sprayed *twice* in one day might feel like. He bolted for home, tail tucked tightly between his legs.

10

Evidence

After downing his dinner of Hearty Hound, Kito hopped on the couch and stretched out. He needed to think, which wasn't easy with Chester yacking away. With his wet beagle nose, he nudged Kito under the chin.

"Just be honest with me," Chester said. "I need to know if you think I have talent. It's always important, when a dog gets famous, to have friends who will be honest with him. So, after watching my tree stunt, think Mighty Mitch will tell the Hollinghorsts that his show can't continue without me? Think they'll just let me join up? I mean, that really would be better than running away with—"

"Chester. I thought you said you weren't going to run away."

"Oh, I won't have to. Barkin' biscuits, I did consider that possibility! But now that I'm certain Mighty Mitch will recognize my talent, well, the Hollinghorsts will just have to give me up, right? For the benefit of the world's entertainment." His beagle body started wagging from his tail to his nose. "I'm just thinking, if I could come up with one or two more stunts, then I'll absolutely seal the deal! Got any ideas?"

Kito closed his eyes, then opened them. "You don't get it. That Mighty Mitch isn't someone you want to travel with. He doesn't let his dogs take breaks until they're desperate. He uses pepper spray on other dogs."

"Well, you must have done something to threaten his show. Probably just made him nervous. I mean, he has his show dogs to protect."

"Chester, what's gotten into you? You'd think that Mighty Mitch was your master already. This showbiz stuff is making you goofy. You're not seeing clearly. He reads a book about dog training with his name on it. I mean, why would he be reading a book he wrote? That doesn't add up. And Bella, a fine little pink poodle—she told me she wants out. And another thing. What do you think happens to dogs when they outlive their usefulness?"

"I'm sure they retire in luxury," Chester said quite seriously.

"Ha. Maybe. And maybe not. I sure wouldn't pin all my hopes on that guy. There's more about him that seems shady than not."

"Liver snaps, Kito! You're just jealous, that's all."

Kito closed his eyes and refused to engage in any more talk. He wasn't going to change his buddy's mind. All he could do was prove that his instincts about Mighty Mitch were right—before it was too late.

Chester pawed at the lakeside door. Mr. Hollinghorst rose from the dinner table and let him outside. No doubt, Chester was heading back to the cedar tree to practice his backflips.

Kito knew he wasn't stunt dog material, but he did have a good mind. If there was ever a time to use his brains, it was now. Then, in a lightning flash of thought, he knew what he had to do. Before he returned to help Bella escape the show, before he figured out how to keep Chester and any other Pembrook dogs from running off with the show, he needed to do *research*.

If Mighty Mitch's Extreme Stunt Dog Show had been on television, had toured everywhere, and was as famous as Mighty Mitch claimed, he should be able to find information on the computer. But when could he get there? From the clink of forks and the smell of barbecued chicken, the Hollinghorsts were still finishing dinner. After that, they usually took their evening walk, which he and Chester were always eager to go on.

He hopped off the couch, trotted upstairs to the master bedroom, and squeezed in through the cracked closet doors. He crept to the back corner, amid dust balls, old shoes, and a pair of wool pants that had fallen to the floor. He circled, settled himself until he was comfortable, put his head on his paws, and waited.

He heard the sounds of dishes being washed in the sink and muffled conversation.

"Nice evening for a walk," Mr. H said.

"Lovely," replied Mrs. H.

The lakeside door slid open. "Chester!" called Mr. H. "C'mon. Let's go for a walk. Kito! Kito!" A pause. "Huh, I thought he was just here, but he must be outside somewhere."

When the house was completely quiet, Kito bolted from the closet, crossed the small landing at the top of the spiral staircase, and trotted into the adjoining studio. Computer research was best to do in the middle of the night, when no one in the world could catch him. But this was an emergency. Fortunately, the computer screen was lit up.

Kito's paws always felt clumsy on the keyboard. Computers were definitely made for humans, not for dogs. But then, as far as he knew, he was the only dog in the world who could read. So, he just had to make do. He tried to use his nails on the keys instead of his paw pads, which always hit too many keys at once.

Within moments he had managed to type in the words needed to find Internet links to Mighty Mitch and his Extreme Stunt Dogs.

But to Kito's amazement, it was the photo of Mighty Mitch that completely threw him. The long white truck with glittering letters was the same. There was a photo of Boomerang, shooting out of a tunnel. But Mighty Mitch was much, much older. He had a white handlebar mustache, a cowboy hat, and a black tuxedo jacket and pants (definitely not shorts). And he wore black shoes, not red sneakers. This Mighty Mitch was old enough to be the father of the man who was handling the stunt dogs in Pembrook.

Kito found another link, and studied several other photos. One photo, in particular, was just what he needed. It was the fake Mighty Mitch in a plain T-shirt and shorts cleaning out a dog cage with a scrub brush and bucket of soapy water. The caption read, "Here, Hector Tripline, son of the famed dog handler, works to keep the show dogs' cages spotless. Each show dog gets plenty of exercise and quality care. Happy dogs make the best stunt dogs!"

He gave a sharp snort of disapproval. So that was it. Dog Watch wasn't dealing with Mighty Mitch, professional dog trainer. They were dealing with his son, Hector. So where was the father? The real trainer?

Kito needed evidence, and it was right there on the screen. He pushed the print button. Then he went back to the photo of the real Mighty Mitch. Again, he pushed print . . . just as the front door opened and the Hollinghorsts returned.

Noiselessly, Kito hopped off the computer chair.

From downstairs, he heard Mr. H say, "What's printing upstairs? That's odd."

Kito had to make a decision, and fast: Hide again, and let the Hollinghorsts wonder about the photos on the printer. Or snatch the photos and then hide, which meant he could get caught in the act of computer piracy. If they had any notion that their dog was smart enough to operate the computer, they might offer him to Mighty Mitch, or a circus, or—heaven forbid—to science for studying.

As Mr. H's footsteps sounded on the staircase, Kito stood on his back legs, snatched the printed photos in his teeth, and nudged them under the carpet. Then he stretched out and rolled back and forth, showing his belly to Mr. H.

"Ha, you silly dog. Of course I'll pet you. You must have bumped a button up here on the computer." Then he squatted beside Kito, gave him a good scratching, and shook his head. "Where were you when we left for our walk? Sleeping?"

Kito shifted on the carpet.

"It's getting late," Mr. H said, reaching over and turning off the computer. "Bedtime for people and dogs."

11

The Photos

Bright and early the next morning, after eating breakfast and being let out to check and mark the yard, Kito returned to the studio. He had to get his paws on the photos he'd printed the evening before.

To his dismay, Mr. H had already settled in at the computer. He was always working on a novel. A dozen published novels lined the shelf above his desk. Mostly mysteries, Kito knew. He would love to read one, but they were always too far from his reach. He had to stick with titles on the lower shelves of bookcases around the house. And he could only read those when everyone was in bed.

It seemed odd that he could read. Somewhere along the way as a puppy he had begun making connections between scribbles and letters. He'd started connecting words on dog food packages and cans with what was inside, and with the words his owners used. Now, strange as it seemed, he could read just about anything as long as he could get his paws on it.

But at this moment, it wasn't his reading ability that concerned him. He had to get the photos out from under the rug. True, he could wait until Mr. H finished writing, or until the deep hours of night, but with the big stunt show one night away, he had to take a few calculated risks.

He sat beside Mr. H, as he often did, then lay down. After a few moments, when Mr. H was nodding to himself and typing like a madman—*clickety, clackety, click, click, click*—Kito nudged his snout ever so quietly under the edge of the rug, felt his nose touch the papers, then snatched them in his teeth. Quickly, quietly, like a lion on the prowl, he made his way with them out of the studio, down the spiral staircase, and trotted to the sliding door.

Standing on the deck beside her easel, Mrs. H was busy brushing layers of paint into a pink-and-orange sunset on canvas. She, too, was likely lost in her work. Kito set down the papers, barked shrilly to be let out and, just as she walked over and opened the door, snatched the papers in his mouth and darted past her.

"Kito—what's that in your mouth? Come back here."

But this was one of those times when he had to pretend he didn't hear her. There were times to be obedient—and times to, well, choose to take action for a greater good.

Just as he reached Pine Street, Chester was at his side. "Chicken gravy! What are you up to?"

"Evidence," Kito said, the photos between

his teeth, "that your hero isn't everything he seems to be."

"Mighty Mitch?" Chester asked.

"Got that right. Only his name isn't Mighty Mitch." Kito didn't slow his pace.

"What?"

"Try Hector. Hector Tripline."

Trotting past the community building, Kito rounded the corner and continued at his doggedly determined pace down the sidewalk of Main Street to the field where the white truck—and Bella—waited.

"I don't get you," Chester complained at his side. "Anything that looks like it might be a good thing, you have to find some reason to judge it as bad. I mean, the way you see things, every floating balloon should probably be popped. And that's exactly what it feels like for me. Here I'm on my way to stardom. My name will be in bright lights! And you can't share my joy. My path to happiness."

Kito glanced at Chester, whose brown eyes were earnest. He meant every word of it. Kito sighed. "Oh, boy."

When they reached the white truck, all was quiet. The obstacle course was still set up, but there was no sign of Hector Tripline or any sound from his dogs. "He probably went out for a fine meal at a local restaurant," Chester said. "Doesn't matter what his name is. A guy like that can afford anything he wants."

Kito ducked under the truck. He found the midsection where he'd communicated with Bella the first time. "Hey, Bella! Anybody in there?"

Silence.

"Well, he probably takes his dogs out to dinner, too," Chester said, nose to the ground and snuffling.

"Bella! Bella!" Kito tried again. He pushed his ear to the truck's floor.

"Mmmm. I'm here," she said. "But I'm so . . . sleepy. I just want to—"

"Bella. Where is the real Mighty Mitch?"

"Home in Arizona. His son's supposed to be watching us, letting us take time off, but—" She yawned audibly. "But he wanted to make some money. Sell his biscuits. Mighty Miscuits." Again, she yawned, long and slow. "I really have to . . . close my eyes."

Something didn't add up. Yesterday, Bella was dashing across the field to talk with him. After spending so much time in the truck, why would she be so sleepy? She should be happy for a visitor! She should be barking and yipping to be let out. If there were a dozen dogs in the truck, it should be noisy—not eerily quiet.

"Does he give you special biscuits?"

"Ummm. Yes. Just before sending us back in the truck. A blue biscuit each."

"Blue? They come in colors?"

"Blue, yes. When we have to be quiet. And"—she yawned again—"and yellow . . . and yell . . ."

Then it was completely silent.

"Bella? C'mon, Bella. Wake up!"

But he couldn't get her to stir again.

"Did you hear that, Chester?"

Snuffle, snuff, snuff. Chester was busy sniffing around the tires at the front of the truck. Then, with a sudden change of course, he pointed himself in the direction of the obstacle course and sniffed his way through tunnels, over and under ladders and hoops. "Gotta practice!" he called.

With meager evidence in his teeth, with paper that was getting increasingly damp from his drool, Kito needed to take action on his own. Dog Watch, the notion of dogs working together, was failing. Maybe, if he could convince one dog in the village that the stunt show needed to be investigated, then perhaps he could rally more dogs to join in. He glanced at the post office across the street. The fire hydrant stood empty. He trotted over and left a simple message: *Dog Watch alert! Meet this morning!*

He turned north down Main Street to find Tundra. She'd know what to do. But when he arrived outside Erickson's Very Fine Grocery Store, Mr. Erickson was loading Tundra into his truck. "Gotta head to the vet to get booster shots for my girl," he said over his shoulder to Kito. Good old Mr. Erickson. He really could read a dog's mind, it seemed. As the truck drove away, Tundra pressed her black nose to the rear window of the truck, as if to apologize.

Next, Kito dashed with the wilting papers to the one other dog he hoped might listen. A dog who had seen enough of the larger world to not think every traveling stunt show was a good thing. And that dog was Bear. Despite the sun quickly warming the morning air, Kito bolted past the post office and up the hill behind it. He took the short-cut. Over the top of the hill he flew, down the now dirt-and-grass-covered sliding hill, past the warming house, and down the street to the white picket fence, which surrounded Angelica Phillips's little yellow house.

Kito pressed his head against the gate, which, thankfully, wasn't latched.

"Bear!" he called. When no answer came, he barked at the front door. If Bear was inside, perhaps his owner would let him out.

"Well, well," came the voice of the local

newspaper reporter. Angelica's hair was pulled up in a bun, and she was barefoot, with orange toenails and matching orange shorts. "Bear," she said, calling over her shoulder, "looks like someone is here to play with you." She studied Kito. "It's early. I haven't even had my coffee yet. "

In no time, Bear was pushing past his owner, tail wagging, tongue hanging. Summers were clearly hard on him with his dense, black, Newfoundland coat. "Kito," he said. "What is it?"

The papers suddenly fell apart and dropped at Kito's feet.

Angelica Phillips reached down and picked them up. "What have we here? You must have been going through someone's garbage, Kito. Or"—she held a few pieces together and studied them—"or through things at Mighty Mitch's truck. Huh. Hard to read, but—well. That must be the father. And, Mighty Mitch—the son? Hmmm. Maybe the father died. Sad."

"No," Kito said. "The father's on vacation!

Mighty Mitch is out to make money with the dogs and sell his biscuits called Mighty Miscuits! And the blue ones make dogs get sleepy. And I bet the yellow biscuits get the dogs hyper to do their stunts."

Angelica Phillips, of course, didn't hear a word of his dog explanation. She stepped back inside with the wilted pieces of paper and closed the screen door behind her.

Bear gave his massive head and body a solid shake. "Kito, if what you're saying is true, then Dog Watch has some work ahead."

"Dog Watch has all but folded," Kito said, leading the way to the shade of the towering spruce. "Up until now, I thought I was the only dog who wasn't starry-eyed about becoming a stunt dog. I left a message at the hydrant for Dog Watch to meet this morning. Bet you and I—and Tundra, when she returns from the vet—are the only ones that will show up."

"Two is better than one," Bear offered. "Let's see if we can strengthen our case before the meeting. Tell me everything you know up to this point."

Kito exhaled with relief, then he began.

Finally, he wasn't feeling so all alone in his suspicions.

12

Gathering Evidence

Within minutes, Bear and Kito marched up and over the sliding hill, and down the other side toward the post office.

"Not a dog in sight yet," Bear said. "Let's hope dogs show up when their owners come to get their mail."

"We have little time left to build our case against Mighty Mitch," Kito said. "Schmitty's gone crazy for fetching. I thought he was going to drown going after a stupid stick. Gunnar only wants to practice his stop-drop-and-roll stunt. And Chester's doing backflips—of all things!"

Before crossing the street to the field, they paused in the shadow of the post office. Kito studied the white truck for movement. The dogs were still in lockdown.

"Well, look at that!" boomed Hector Tripline's voice. "Ain't you something?"

To the right and across the railroad tracks, Hector was standing outside the door to Grandma's Pantry. At his feet, Gunnar rolled over and over, then sat up, wagging his tail.

Then Hector turned away—"Time for pancakes!"—and headed inside.

Bear lumbered into motion and crossed the street toward the truck. "Couldn't be a better time for a little looking around."

First thing, Kito slipped underneath the truck. "Bella!" he called.

But no answer came in return.

By now she was probably in an unreachable sleep.

Kito slipped to the other side of the truck. To his amazement, when he circled around the long vehicle, he found the passenger door cracked open. Hector must have forgotten to give it a good slam shut.

With his snout, Kito wedged his head inside until the door creaked wider. Then he jumped up on the floorboards and sniffed around. Before he knew it, Bear was right there beside him, sitting on the seat behind the wheel.

"Hey, Kito."

"Yeah?" Kito kept snooping through empty coffee cups and sheets of paper mixed with discarded candy bar wrappers, hoping to find something valuable.

"Ever wonder what it must feel like to drive a truck? I mean, wouldn't it be great to go down the road in a big rig like this?"

The sight of Bear behind the wheel would have been almost comical if they'd had time to play around. "Bear. We've got work to do. But yes, it would be fun."

For a moment, Bear didn't move, as if he

would pretend forever to be driving a truck. But then he stretched his neck, pulled down the visor with his paw, and out slipped a few pieces of paper. They fluttered down to Kito, right in front of his eyes. He didn't want to let on about his reading ability. It was one thing to be a smart dog, but another to be show-offy. Not only that, but a dog that could read might be put in a circus show—or a stunt show. No, it was better to keep his reading skill to himself. He studied the papers carefully, just long enough to see two important facts: The larger paper had the words "truck registration" and a name after "owner."

"Papers, papers," Kito said. "Maybe they hold clues about who this truck really belongs to." He picked up a small white card in his teeth. "And this could be a business card—with useful information. The kind of thing a dog like you could deliver to your owner, perhaps?"

"What about the biscuits?" Bear asked. "If we could find those, we'd be getting closer to proving—"

"Hey! What in the blasted world are you dogs doing in my truck?!"

Before Kito risked pepper spray, he bolted out the door and right through the legs of Hector, knocking the imposter over. Kito didn't stop running until he crossed the street and reached the fire hydrant.

When he glanced back, Bear was right behind him, papers ruffling at the edges of his teeth.

"If it's okay with you," Bear said, "I'm gettin' these to my owner before I get them too slobber-soaked. Maybe Angelica will know what to do with them. Might be something, right?"

Kito was more than pleased. "Definitely something. See what she has to say."

Emergency Hydrant
Meeting

Within minutes, dogs—and owners collecting their mail—began to show up at the fire hydrant. One sniff, and the dogs turned to Kito.

"Emergency meetin'?" Muffin asked, twirling on her back legs. "I'm fixin' to be the top choice at tonight's big show! Hope I don't hurt y'all's feelings."

"Hey, old chum!" Chester bounded toward the hydrant ahead of Mr. and Mrs. H. "Only hours left to go before tonight's show!"

Kito groaned.

Shortly, Tundra, Schmitty, and Lucky gathered around.

Tundra turned toward Kito, her back hairs flagged. White and stately, she liked to remind the dogs, daily, who was the alpha. Kito's tail dropped between his legs. It was important at such times to show a little respect, otherwise Tundra might attack him with her teeth.

He cowered, lowered himself halfway to the ground, and approached her. She stood tall. "Kito. You've requested a meeting."

"Yes."

She relaxed her stance, settled onto her back haunches, and said, "Good. Fine. I don't see a reason to wait for more dogs to arrive. Fill us in." Just then, Bear returned.

Kito drew a breath, settled back into his skin, and told everything he could about Hector Tripline. He relayed about the Gratitude Program, about being attacked with pepper spray, about Bella's complaints of mistreatment and wanting to escape, and about the photos and truck papers.

"Bear," Tundra asked, "you said you

delivered papers to your owner, Angelica Phillips?"

"That's right. I set them on the porch step where she couldn't miss them."

"And?"

"I don't know. When she left for work just now, the papers were gone. I hope she took them and they didn't just blow away."

"One more thing," Kito added. "The biscuits! Mighty Miscuits is what he calls them. Bella said that he gives the dogs blue biscuits to get them to be quiet. And they work! I couldn't wake Bella up, once they took hold."

Tundra rose and paced around their tight circle. "Sleeping biscuits? This is disturbing."

"Sleeeep is gooood," Gunnar volunteered. He shook his head back and forth, sending a slippery string of slime flying. It landed right on the top of the Raggedy Ann–painted hydrant.

"Sleep is good when it's *voluntary*," Schmitty said. "I wouldn't want someone drugging me with biscuits to make me sleepy. That's an indignity to dogs every-where."

"True, dogs should be dogs," Chester agreed. "However, there are dogs who sometimes come from lesser breeding. Dogs that lack AKC registration perhaps need to be medicated with special biscuits."

Schmitty growled, and so did Kito. They both tackled Chester until he rolled over twice and settled on his back, legs up. "Criminy! I was just making a point, that's all."

"A low, insensitive point," Kito said. "I'm a chow chow mix. You think I should be given special biscuits to make me sleep? You think Schmitty should be? He's a purebred Labrador retriever. He just doesn't have papers."

"Enough!" Tundra commanded. "Let's get back on track here. We seem to have mounting concerns, but nothing solid. Nothing that can actually stop this Hector Tripline from continuing on just exactly as he's doing. He'll do his evening stunt show and head to the next town."

"Unless Dog Watch stops him," Schmitty

said. He looked around knowingly at the other dogs, this time without the smile that so frequently accompanied his friendly attitude. "I've been practicing my retrieving skills and had hoped to impress the—"

"Meeee toooo," Gunnar added. "I'm gonnnnnna shoooow my stunt."

Schmitty shook his floppy ears. "What I'm trying to say is, those of us who have been practicing our stunts will have a chance to be inside the stunt show fence. When that time comes, we could come up with a plan to locate those biscuits."

Bear stepped solidly into the circle's center. He sat tall and proud.

The other dogs hushed, waiting.

"I don't have a stunt," Bear said. "But I have a hearty physique."

"A what?" Schmitty asked.

"I'm a big, healthy, strong dog," he said. "I'm saying, once we locate the supply of Mighty Miscuits, we need a Dog Watch member to be the willing *victim*. The science experiment."

"Good giblets!" Chester complained. "You're losing me. What on earth are you saying?"

"I'm saying . . . if I eat too many Mighty Miscuits, they'll probably make me sick. Hopefully not sick enough to kill me—"

"Kill yooooou?" Gunnar said. "Nooooo!"

Bear turned to Gunnar. "As I said, hopefully not. But sick enough to get the attention of my owner and the rest of the villagers."

Bear was as tall as Tundra, and nearly twice the weight. He was three times as heavy as Kito. If any dog should take such chances, Kito agreed that Bear was the likely candidate. Still, it made him feel sick to think that one of their very own Dog Watch members should have to take such dire risks.

"Bear," Kito said. "I admire your willingness to step forward. But between now and tonight's show, we must do absolutely everything possible to minimize such risks to you. We need to act as a team—and heaven knows we have little time left."

Bear lowered his head toward Kito.

"Thank you. But I owe all of you my life. If you hadn't found me in that winter den, I would have died. You dogs saved me. And that's why . . . this is a risk I'm willing to take."

14

The Big Show

At mid-afternoon, the newspaper arrived on time in the able hands of Howie. "Hi! Hi! Hi!" he shouted from his bike. He tossed the newspaper toward the front door, where Kito and Chester were sitting. The headline caught Kito's interest immediately: FAMOUS STUNT DOG SHOW TONIGHT IN PEMBROOK.

From the basket between the handlebars, Howie grabbed treats. "Here! Here! Here!" he called, and threw the biscuits to the dogs.

Kito flinched. The snacks dropped at his

feet. With all the talk about Mighty Miscuits, he wasn't as quick to eat these bone-shaped treats. But then he came to his senses, snatched up the snacks, and gulped them down. As Howie's bike squeaked away, Kito knew he would never have to worry that Howie would give him something harmful.

"Good buddy!" Chester looked at Kito. "I figure I have just a few more hours to practice my stunts. So if you don't mind—" And in a flash of brown and white, Chester raced at the nearest phone pole, ran up it a few feet, and did his backflip.

"I'll admit," Kito called, "it's a good stunt. But I hope you're not still holding out hope of traveling with the show."

"I'm keeping my options open," Chester said. "Whatever happened to innocent until proven guilty?" He charged the pole again.

Kito trotted off down Pine Street. "I'll be back soon." As he passed Schmitty's house, he could hear the distant sound of Hillary's words across the water. "Good boy, Schmitty! There it is. Fetch it up!"

When Kito neared the field and the obstacle course, he headed well out of view of Hector, who was lounging again in the shade of his truck awning, drink in hand. By steering wide to the east, around the post office, and swinging wide to the north, alongside empty railroad tracks, then following the tracks west, he was able to come up to the truck from behind. Hector didn't have a clue as Kito edged under the truck.

"Bella!" he shouted. Thank goodness dogs could shout to each other without barking.

"Kito," came the reply. "Darling, have you figured out how I'm going to escape yet?"

"Yes, we have a few plans to bring Hector to justice. I just wanted you to know that, um, we're working on it."

"You don't sound entirely confident," she replied.

"I'm not. But Dog Watch has come through before, and I promise we're going to do everything we can to help your situation."

"I don't know. I'm getting pretty discouraged. . . ."

"Trust me," Kito said, with more conviction than he actually felt, but he needed to give Bella hope. "Trust Dog Watch."

Hector stirred and swung around. He leaned over the edge of his chair and peered at Kito. "You!"

In the sprint of his lifetime—with the speed of a stunt dog—Kito bounded home. He arrived, out of breath, with a sense that maybe, just maybe, justice would soon be closing around that man.

"Ladies and gentlemen! Boys and girls!" Hector strutted once again around his white-fence enclosure. His dogs waited in the nearby tent. From all the wiggling inside the purple tent walls, Kito suspected the dogs' diet had been switched recently from blue biscuits to yellow.

"The dogs of the Extreme Stunt Dog Show are eager to go! Eager to show you their stuff! So now, all the way from Hollywood, comes—Tornado!"

Just as in the preview show, the tiny dog zipped through the tunnels, over ladders, and through hoops. When he finished, he bounded toward Hector, bounced off his chest, and did the obstacle course again—in reverse!

But this time, when Kito watched, he felt none of the earlier excitement about the show. Next, Hector introduced Boomerang, who did more Frisbee tricks. And then Hector introduced Stella, a lanky greyhound that he clocked as she raced the fence's perimeter. "Your cheering will only make her go faster!"

The villagers clapped and whistled and cheered. Indeed, Stella appeared to double, then triple her speed. Kito had never witnessed such a fast dog!

"Yellow biscuits," he whispered to Bear and Chester, who were on each side of him, seated by their owners on the bottom row of bleachers.

"You can bet on that," Bear said.

"Maybe," Chester said. "It's still all theory at this point. Just might be that this whole stunt show is the real thing. And if so, you know where I'm headin' when it's done. California. Hollywood! I'm keeping my options open, that's what!"

Kito and Bear exchanged doubtful glances.

Between stunts, Hector toned down his approach. "Friends," he said, with a generous stretch of his arms and hands to the audience. "The dogs of this show are treated only with kindness. I call it my 'Gratitude Program.' The more your dogs feel appreciated, the more they are eager to perform stunts to their best ability. And that's why, at the beginning of every show, I reward my dogs with Mighty Miscuits!" He waved a bright yellow dog biscuit in the air. "Yes, folks! Mighty Miscuits! Created from only the finest natural ingredients to keep your dog healthy. Whether they're full of zip, or calm and sleepy, Mighty Miscuits can help your dog be the dog you've always dreamed of owning!" From his back pocket he produced a royal blue biscuit.

"I'm proud to introduce these new products, and at the end of this show, you good people of Pembrook will have a chance to purchase your own supply. It's a one-time offer: a bag of blue and a bag of yellow—each for the low, low price of $19.95." He walked back and forth in front of the audience, then stopped abruptly and squared his fists to his hips. "But, wait! For you, I'll make a very special, one-time offer. I'll give you two bags"—he held up two fingers—"that's two, for the unbelievably low price of $19.95."

A murmur went up from the crowd.

Kito glanced over his shoulder. Even Mr. and Mrs. H appeared to be discussing the biscuits. He couldn't believe this. These biscuits could ruin dogs everywhere! They'd become robot dogs without the ability to think or behave on their own, ever again. Just behind Bear, Angelica Phillips was scribbling madly in her notepad. Was she caught up in the Mighty Miscuit excitement too? If the Dog Watch plan failed, every dog in Pembrook might become a victim of Mighty Miscuits, only making this imposter richer!

Kito growled at Mighty Mitch, who had paused directly in from of him. "Ah, this dog. We've met before. He would be a fine candidate for a steady diet of blue calming Mighty Miscuits!"

The crowd chuckled, but Kito didn't find anything funny in the words.

"Kito," Mr. H whispered, pulling Kito closer by the collar, "settle down now. It's just showbiz. You don't need to act like a guard dog."

The show continued. Mighty Mitch brought out three small dogs who were expert Frisbee catchers. They jumped for any and every Frisbee that he tossed: over his head, over his stomach, lying down and in the air, jumping over his back and catching them in the air, through hoops, during backflips. . . .

"Wow," Chester said.

Low Frisbees and ultra-high Frisbees—the little dogs caught them all, and the crowd went wild with applause.

"Where's Bella?" Bear asked.

"I don't know," Kito said. "I thought she was in the show too."

As soon as the tiny dogs finished, Hector sent them back to the tent. He wiped beads of sweat from his head. "Now, folks, I promised to consider the talent right here in Pembrook before heading with the Extreme Stunt Dog Show to the next eager town."

"Should I snatch them from his hand right now?" Bear asked.

"No," Kito advised. "Just wait."

Bear's mouth watered. Kito knew the symptoms. He wasn't yearning for biscuits. His mouth was watering the way some dogs' mouths do before being carsick. Bear, despite his bravery, was likely dreading what was ahead. And who could blame him?

"Chester," Kito whispered, "promise you won't forget your part in Dog Watch, no matter how much applause you get out there."

But Chester was staring straight ahead, wiggling with anticipation.

Blue and Yellow Biscuits

"Well, folks," Mighty Mitch said, parading around in his long tuxedo tails, shorts, and red sneakers, "that's nearly it for our show. Just a reminder: Don't forget that this is your one and only chance to buy your very own Mighty Miscuits. Cash only, however."

Kito strained against his collar, but Mr. H continued to hold him fast. He wished he could go poke his nose into the holding tent and find Bella.

The music from the speaker went louder in volume. *Bum-bum-bumba-bum! Bum-*

bum-bumba-bum! "But let's close on an elegant note first. Now, for the one and only ballet-dancing dog, let's hear it for—" The music continued. It was hardly ballet music. "Bella!"

The crowd applauded. A few people whistled shrilly.

From the door of the holding tent, Bella twirled round and round on her hind legs toward Hector. Her silver skirt sparkled as she twirled.

"Oh, my," pined Muffin from the sidelines. "That's a mighty fine outfit!"

"Is that a dog?" Bear asked.

"It's Bella," Kito said. "Don't let that outfit and pink fur throw you. She's a good dog, right down to her paws."

The crowd clapped as she rounded a turn with each loud beat. Round and round and round she twirled, snapping her head in the direction of Hector with each spin. Then, only a few steps from Hector, in an apparent change of program, she dropped to her feet and rounded on all fours toward the tails of the tuxedo. In a flash of tiny white teeth, she jumped and, with a growl, locked down on the imposter's backside.

"Bella! Ouch! Ouch! Ouch!" Now Hector was whirling and twirling on the toes of his red sneakers. The flaps of his coattails were extended like swallow tails in flight. With each twirl, Bella hung on, her body extended straight out from her teeth to the tip of her pink poodle tail.

"Go, Bella!" Kito shouted. He began barking and yipping too, to cheer her on.

The crowd laughed and clapped, as if this part of the show had been planned. Finally, Bella let go and toppled away to the ground, but picked herself back up, yipped proudly, and raced back to the holding tent.

"Get back here you little—" Hector said, fist raised toward the tent. Then he seemed to catch himself and he turned, forcing a smile to the audience.

"Well, folks, hope you enjoyed that grand finale!"

The villagers clapped louder still.

"I, um, er . . ." Hector faltered. "I guess we'll just move right along, then. Time for local dogs to show off their talent! C'mon down!"

This was the part of the program that Kito hoped would go as planned. With stardom still glittering in Chester's eyes, he wasn't at all sure.

Four dogs trotted out onto the field: Gunnar, Chester, Schmitty, and Muffin.

"Sit," Hector told them all.

They all sat.

"Well, that's a good start!" He laughed. "Okay, dogs. Do your tricks!"

The four dogs sat there.

"Go!" Hector called.

The dogs looked at one another.

"I don't know what he wants, do you?" Chester called to the other dogs.

"You see, folks," Hector said, "they need a little motivation." He pulled yellow biscuits from his pocket.

"Don't eat those!" Kito called.

One by one, he tossed the dogs biscuits, and one by one, they gulped them down.

"Okay now, with Mighty Miscuits, do your stuff!"

Gunnar started twitching, Chester started itching his belly with his hind leg, Muffin wiggled and turned in circles, and Schmitty started jumping up and down in place. Cheering erupted.

"Give it just a minute more," Hector called out to the audience.

Seconds slipped by, when in an explosion of energy, Gunnar started running around the perimeter of the white enclosure. Running! Schmitty raced into one of the tunnels, then kept going in and out, over and over and over. Muffin did what she does best. She danced on her back legs, almost as well as Bella had done. And Chester, he ran up Hector's chest and backflipped. Then he took off and ran up the side of the truck and backflipped. But with this backflip, a hinged cupboard on the outside wall of the truck dropped down to reveal a display of Mighty Miscuits. Bags of blue biscuits and bags of yellow biscuits lined the built-in cupboard.

"Looks like the dogs have found their energy—and talent!" Hector called. "Let's give them a big hand!"

Suddenly, Bear bolted away from Angelica Phillips with his leash trailing behind him. He raced straight across the obstacle course for the biscuits. He reached up on his long back legs and pulled down a blue bag of Mighty Miscuits.

"That's it! Show's over!" Hector's back was turned toward the truck as he faced the audience. "Thanks, dogs, for participating, and now, owners, it's time to buy your very own Mighty Miscuits, which it looks like Pembrook dogs already love!"

In unison, Kito and every other dog of Dog Watch escaped from their owners' leashes. When a dog really needs to escape, he finds a way. Kito did the old pull-and-twist-away technique, which freed him completely of both collar and leash in one quick motion. He dashed with the other dogs straight to where Bear was munching blue biscuits.

Angelica Phillips sped across the field too.

She squatted beside Bear, whose lips were blue with biscuits.

"Bear! What have you done? No, no, no! Come with me. You other dogs. No!"

The dogs sat back on their haunches. Kito was glad she'd said something. They might have forgotten that the biscuits were supposed to be off-limits.

In a huge groan, Bear dropped to the ground, his legs splayed beneath him. Angelica cried out, "Bear!" Then she jumped up, rounded on Hector, and shouted, "What's in those biscuits, anyway? Look at my dog!"

Kito had seen Angelica Phillips angry before, and it wasn't pretty.

Her eyebrows furrowed. "Shame on you!" Then she dropped to her knees and pulled Bear's head into her lap. He was out cold.

In the midst of all the commotion, a *stranger* appeared. As if stepping out of a movie, a towering, white-haired man in a white tuxedo, white top hat, and white cane stormed from the bleachers and crossed the field. Kito noticed that just beyond the bleachers, a limousine waited, its driver at the wheel.

Everyone, villagers and dogs, turned their gaze toward this stranger.

"Hector, Hector!" the man boomed, taking long, determined strides.

Usually Kito bristled at the sight of any stranger, but this stranger didn't make him bristle at all. He knew the face from the photo. This was the real Mighty Mitch Tripline, the real dog trainer, and father of Hector.

16

Pops

Suddenly scratching his forehead as if he'd just been infested with fleas, Hector shifted back and forth on his feet. "Pops," he said, "what, um, brings you here?"

"Let's just say a little bird told me," said the tall gentleman, glancing over toward Angelica Phillips, who nodded back at him. "Let's just say I took the first flight out this morning to see your show."

"Uh-huh." The scratching was turning Hector's forehead red.

"And I didn't like what I saw one bit,

Hector. Mighty Miscuits? What in the world are you up to, son? Dog training isn't about quick money or quick fixes! Here I'm supposed to be taking two months off to rest. The dogs are supposed to be getting the best possible care—and rest, let me remind you—while staying with you at the family kennels in California. And you're here? In Pembrook, Minnesota?!"

"But . . . I . . ."

A police car pulled forward alongside the curb, between the field and the post office. A bowlegged officer stepped out, carrying a pair of handcuffs.

"Is this the young man you told me about?" he asked, approaching the gathering.

Mighty Mitch Tripline nodded his head. "Yes, sir. Sure is. Stole my truck and my stunt dogs. A little time at your fine hotel, Officer, might be a good thing."

"You intend to press charges?"

"Yes, sir. I do."

"Oh, Pops!"

"Don't 'Oh, Pops' me, Hector. You're a

grown man now. You should know better. We'll talk tomorrow. You think about all this at the local jail."

Head down, Hector walked with the officer to the police car. When he was settled in the backseat, they started off. Hector looked back once. Kito glared at him. But the only thing Hector seemed to be looking at were his rows and rows of Mighty Miscuits.

As the police car headed off in the direction of the county jail, Mighty Mitch Tripline turned to the display shelves and stuffed the bags of blue and yellow biscuits into huge, black garbage bags. Then he handed them to Mayor Jorgenson. "See that they're destroyed, please."

The mayor nodded.

"Thanks for your help too," Mighty Mitch continued "in alerting me to this scandal. My own son . . . I can't tell you how apologetic I feel about this whole mess."

Mayor Jorgenson bowed slightly, the evening sun glistening on his bald head. "Couldn't have done it without our local reporter looking into some mysterious photos and information that just didn't add up."

Mighty Mitch Tripline kneeled beside Bear. "Get your dog to the vet. This could be serious."

Angelica snapped open her cell phone, made a quick call, and said, "Yes, I'll meet you there. Thank you!"

Then, with the help of Mr. and Mrs. H, Hillary Rothchild, Harry Erickson, and others, she loaded Bear in the back of her car and sped off in the direction of the vet's clinic.

"Now, to check on my dogs." The lanky and distinguished father of Hector headed for the holding tent. He let out the eight performers, who jumped and zipped around the obstacle course. After rounds and rounds, his dogs began to slow their pace somewhat and started to greet the Pembrook dogs.

Mighty Mitch Tripline shook his head. "Way too hyped up."

Kito sat off on the sidelines. He watched this newcomer with growing appreciation. Not all strangers were bad.

While the star dogs ran around, Mighty Mitch Tripline opened the back door of the show truck. In a few moments he was back outside.

"Until they wake up," he said to the villagers who hovered around, piecing events together, "I have four sleep-drugged dogs."

In his hands he carried a tattered copy of his training book. "Hmmm. He underlined everything here about my Gratitude Program. But he sure didn't put it into practice!" The moment he stepped out toward the obstacle course, his eight awake dogs, including Bella, ran to his side. When he squatted down beside them, they were a tangle of hugs and scratching. And the dogs, Kito noticed, slipped in several welcoming kisses on the real Mighty Mitch's face.

"I promise," he told his dogs, "this will never, ever happen again. Now you're going to get some real time off from performances. But not with Hector. I'll be driving you straight to Arizona. You'll all come and live in the vacation home with me and the missus."

Mighty Mitch Tripline, of course, couldn't hear all the chatter between his dogs, but Kito did. He was standing close enough to catch a few phrases.

"So glad to be rescued!" said a tiny charcoal dog.

"Our real master is back—at last!"

"Good riddance to that loser!" cried Bella.

Kito piped up. "At least you gave him a good biting farewell!"

"Sure did, darling."

17

A Mighty Farewell

"Dog Watch!" Tundra called from the fire hydrant the next morning. She barked and barked until nearly every dog showed up. The post office wasn't even open yet, but that didn't matter.

Once the dogs, including Kito and Chester had settled, Tundra walked in and out amidst her pack. "Job well done," she said. "Dog Watch worked together yesterday to get a scoundrel put in jail."

Kito knew that they'd just barely figured out a plan in time, and that they'd certainly needed the extra help of Bear's owner, who had been quick to do her own research and alert Mighty Mitch Tripline that all was not well with his stunt dogs.

"I've heard through my owner, Mr. Erickson, that there will be a special farewell celebration at noon." Tundra pointed her snout across the street, toward the field where the white truck was still parked. "And I hear that there will be some sort of public apology made by Hector. I suggest that it would be good form for us to show our support for these stunt dogs by attending."

"Here, here!" Chester said.

The other dogs looked at him, brows raised.

"That's what they say in Parliament," Chester went on. "You know, in England! I've heard it on the news, when the members shout out, 'Here! Here!' in agreement. I'm just saying a big *yes* to what Tundra just said."

"Here! Here!" the dogs said in unison. Then they grew more excited and started yipping, barking, and howling until Mavis, the postmaster, stepped out of the post office with a folded flag in her hands. "What's the matter with you dogs?! Pipe down!"

The dogs settled back into sniffs and wags.

Then Mavis walked over to the empty flagpole, fastened the flag, pulled on the rope, and hoisted it high. Before she stepped back into the post office, she wedged her hands on her hips and her gray postmaster shorts. "If you ask me," she said, "you dogs have lives that are so much better than any of those show dogs could ever have."

The dogs wagged their tails. The postmaster smiled, perhaps the only one she would offer up to anyone all day. Tundra leaned into Mavis's muscular legs and let Mavis scratch her under the collar. "I'd swear," Mavis said, looking around at the dogs, "some days you all seem like you're actually up to something. Solving mysteries or some such." She chuckled to herself, then turned away and headed up the steps into the post office.

The dogs of Dog Watch trotted across the street, passed the empty, fenced field, and raced ahead to the bay and Seven Oaks Park. They romped and wrestled, chasing one another across an ancient log onshore. They drank thirstily from the cool, clear lake. And when a long train rumbled across the lift bridge from Canada into the United States, they paused to watch it pass through their village.

Life *was* good, Kito had to agree. Dog Watch had helped right the wrongs for the traveling stunt dogs. They'd been key in alerting the authorities to Hector's practices. And in the process, he'd made a friend in Bella.

He glanced over toward the field. Mighty Mitch Tripline was just letting all his dogs outside. A dozen dogs of all sizes ran around the enclosure. The real Mighty Mitch laughed as the dogs caught Frisbees and ran the obstacle course. He praised them with "Good dog!" and "That-a-way!" He patted them on their heads, and scratched their bellies when they flopped at his feet.

Kito trotted up to the plastic fence. Bella saw him and darted over to meet him. They touched noses.

"I heard our trainer say that after Hector makes an apology here, he'll be on the next flight back to his home in California."

"That's good. But doesn't he pay a penalty or serve jail time or anything?"

"Darling, sometimes family ties run deep. The real Mighty Mitch has a big, big heart. He didn't want his son locked away, so he's dropping the charges. But it's clear Hector will not have anything to do with us again. Sounds like he'll go back to what he loves to do most."

"What's that?"

"Surfing, I guess."

"But what if he tries selling his biscuits again?"

Bella shook her pink fuzzy head. "Not a chance. From the phone conversation I over-heard, if he even tries to do something like that again, his father will definitely press charges and make sure they stick."

"Well, maybe that's good enough. It's something."

"We're doing a bonus show at noon today as a thank-you to Pembrook for being so helpful. Then it's off to Arizona. Will you watch us?"

At that moment, Chester scooted up to Kito's side. He pressed himself between Kito and the fence so that he was standing closer to Bella. "Another show? Did you see my backflip? What did you think? Got any ideas for how I can improve it? Think I've got the right stuff?"

"The right stuff?" she repeated. She glanced around. "Road life isn't easy. But it's all I know. If I were you, I think I'd just soak up the freedom you have and enjoy it. Darling, that backflip of yours—only one word fits: *divine!*"

When the noontime show was over, Mighty Mitch Tripline loaded up his Extreme Stunt Dog Show equipment and his amazing dogs. He waved good-bye from the driver's window of his sleek truck. The words "Extreme Stunt Show" glittered like a thousand diamonds in the afternoon sun.

Kito glanced up and down Main Street. Gunnar was wandering off to the tavern, likely in search of pretzels and pizza. Muffin rode in her owner's bike basket, her head high, toward the beach. Schmitty trotted home alongside his owner, Hillary Rothchild, whose fingernails, Kito had noticed earlier, were perpetually green from gardening. And Bear, now feeling much better, sat at the feet of Angelica Phillips as she snapped a final photograph of the truck heading down the road.

Life in Pembrook wasn't flashy. It wasn't glittery or filled with showbiz. But it was— Kito knew to the depths of his paws—truly good.

"C'mon, buddy," he said.

And together, he and Chester trotted off toward home.